Disney's

THE LITTLE
MERMAID

It was the day that all the undersea kingdom had been awaiting. Princess Ariel, the Little Mermaid, was going to make her singing debut. Her father, King Triton, was particularly proud. Ariel had the most beautiful voice in the undersea world according to Sebastian, the crab. Sebastian was the castle's music director.

Ariel's older sisters began the concert, but when a giant seashell opened to reveal the Little Mermaid, Ariel was nowhere to be found.

"Ariel!" King Triton roared.

As usual, Ariel was exploring a sunken ship with her friend Flounder. She loved collecting objects from the human world. Today, she found a fork.

She took it to Scuttle, the sea gull, to find out what it was. "It's a dinglehopper," he declared. "Humans use these babies to straighten their hair."

Suddenly, Ariel remembered the concert.

"Oh my gosh!" she cried, and swam home as fast as she could. She didn't know that Ursula, the Sea Witch, was watching. King Triton had banished Ursula from the palace long ago, and now she was plotting revenge.

As Ariel had feared, her father was furious
that she had missed the concert because she
had been exploring a sunken ship. "You are
never to have anything to do with humans
again. Never!" he commanded.

"Maybe she needs someone to keep an eye on
her," King Triton decided when Ariel had left.
He chose Sebastian for the job.

Sebastian followed Ariel to the grotto where
she kept her treasures. Moments later, Ariel
spotted a dark shape high above. "A ship!" she
cried, as she swam for the surface.

"No, Ariel!" called Sebastian. But Ariel never
looked back.

Ariel had seen many ships before. But this was the first time she was able to swim close enough to see the humans onboard. They were having a birthday party for someone named Prince Eric.

When darkness came, the sailors lit up the sky with fireworks. But no one, except a big sheepdog named Max, noticed Ariel.

Prince Eric received a statue of himself as a birthday gift. "It's really something," he said in thanks, though he was secretly embarrassed by the huge replica of himself.

The humans were having such a good time, that no one noticed the black clouds approaching the ship. In an instant, a great storm struck.

The sailors jumped into a lifeboat, but Eric swam back to rescue Max.

Ariel watched Eric lower the dog to safety. Then a huge explosion threw Eric into the sea. Ariel plunged beneath the water to save him.

The storm had passed when Scuttle saw Ariel drag the unconscious Eric onto the beach.

"Look! He's breathing," Ariel said. "Oh, he's so beautiful!"

At that moment, she knew she loved Eric. She began to sing. Eric's eyelids fluttered.

Suddenly Ariel heard Max bark, and knew that Prince Eric's friends would soon find him.

When Eric opened his eyes, Ariel was gone. But the sound of her voice was still in his ears.

When King Triton found out that Ariel had gone to the surface and met a human, he went straight to her grotto to find her. "You disobeyed me!" he shouted. As punishment, he blasted Ariel's treasures to bits — including the statue of Eric which Flounder had saved for her.

Ursula watched the destruction from her palace, and gloated with pleasure.

"I think the time is ripe," she said to her two slippery hench-eels, Flotsam and Jetsam.

Following Ursula's instructions, Flotsam and Jetsam slithered to Ariel's cave, and hissed, "We know someone who can help you." Ariel followed them to the Sea Witch's den.

"The solution to your problem is simple, my dear," Ursula purred. "You must become a human."

"But how?" Ariel asked.

"Just sign this contract," Ursula said.

"Don't listen to her!" Sebastian warned.

"I love Eric. This is the only way," Ariel replied. So she signed Ursula's contract, and traded her beautiful voice for a human body.

She had only three days to win Eric's love. If she failed, she would belong to Ursula forever.

Soon after signing the contract, Ariel was lying on a beach, and Scuttle was staring at her new legs in wonder. "Ariel's not a mermaid anymore," Sebastian explained.

Prince Eric had been searching for the girl
with the unforgettable voice. When he found
Ariel, he hoped she was the one. But she could
not speak, much less sing, so he decided she
wasn't.

Still, this beautiful girl needed help. Eric
invited her to be his guest, and soon found
himself falling in love with her, just as Ariel
had hoped.

But then Ursula showed up. She had disguised
herself as a beautiful girl named Vanessa, and
wore Ariel's voice in a locket around her neck.

"That voice," Eric said when he heard it. "It's
you — my one true love!"

Eric made up his mind to marry
Vanessa at sea that very day. But
when Scuttle looked in the ship's
window and saw Vanessa's
reflection in her mirror, he realized
she was really the Sea Witch!

Scuttle organized a flock of birds
and sea creatures to attack Vanessa.
The locket broke from Vanessa's
neck and released Ariel's voice to
its rightful owner.

"Oh Eric . . . " Ariel said.

"It was you all the time!" Eric
exclaimed.

But it was too late. "You belong to
me now," the Sea Witch screamed
at Ariel.

As the sun set, Ariel's three days were up. The wedding guests stared in shock as she became a mermaid again. In a moment, she and Ursula vanished beneath the waves.

Back under the sea, Ursula showed Ariel's father the signed contract. "However, I'll give Ariel her freedom — in exchange for yours," she said.

King Triton loved his little daughter so much that he agreed to the bargain.

"At last!" Ursula crowed. "I am sole ruler of all the ocean!"

Suddenly, Prince Eric's harpoon flashed through the water, wounding the Sea Witch.

Ursula raised her trident and aimed it at Eric. But Ariel managed to throw Ursula off balance, so that the Sea Witch hit her own evil eels instead of Eric.

Ursula was so enraged that her evil heart grew.
And so did she, until she towered over the
ocean. "You pitiful fools!" she shrieked. "Now
you will feel the power of the Sea Witch!"

Lightning flashed. Great waves swept over the
sea, tossing up ancient shipwrecks from the
seabed.

Eric managed to climb onto one of the wrecks, and steered the sharp bowsprit straight at the Sea Witch. With a bloodcurdling scream, she disintegrated into a patch of bubbling black ooze.

As soon as Triton regained his power as king of the sea, he went searching for his daughter. He found her staring longingly at Eric, who had been washed safely onto the beach.

King Triton granted Ariel her dearest wish. He made her human forever, so that she could marry Prince Eric.

The wedding was held onboard Eric's ship, with all the merpeople looking on from the sea.

Though King Triton was sad to know his Little Mermaid would no longer live with him under the sea, his heart was lightened knowing that she would be forever happy with the man of her dreams.